Let's Try It, and Buy It!

T0321488

Written by Michaela Morgan

Illustrated by Laura Arias

Collins

Who and what is in this story?

Listen and say

Download the audio at www.collins.co.uk/839761

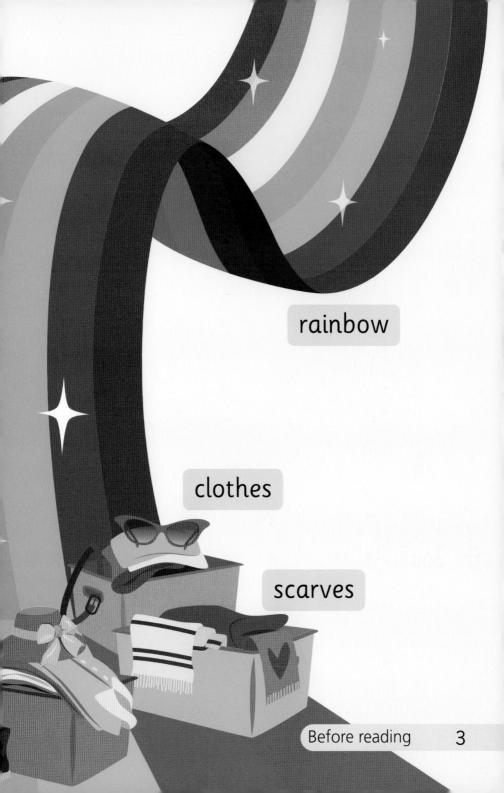

rainbow

clothes

scarves

Sid says, "Hats! Scarves! Shoes!
I like this shop!"

Sid

The woman says, "Hello, children. Try these! They're nice."

The woman says, "They look great! Do you want them?"

No, thank you!

Sid asks, "Can I try this jacket?"

Sid asks, "Can I try those trousers?"

They're too big!

Now, a hat.

Anna says, "I love these trousers and this skirt."

Anna says, "And scarves! This scarf and this scarf!

Anna says, "Let's see. I need seven!"

Seven scarves!
Seven?

Anna says, "Yes. A red scarf and a green scarf."

Anna says, "And yellow, orange, blue, purple and pink scarves. Great!"

Oh!

Sid says, "Can I try that hat and those shoes, please?"

They're very big!

Sid says, "Wow! I think they're great!"

Anna and Sid can go to the birthday lunch now!

And I'm a rainbow!

19

Red, yellow, pink and blue.
Orange, purple and green!

Anna is a rainbow!
Sid looks funny!

Happy Birthday!

Picture dictionary

Listen and repeat

hat

jacket

rainbow

scarf

shoes

trousers

1 Look and order the story

2 Listen and say

Collins

Published by Collins
An imprint of HarperCollins*Publishers*
Westerhill Road
Bishopbriggs
Glasgow
G64 2QT

HarperCollins*Publishers*
1st Floor, Watermarque Building
Ringsend Road
Dublin 4
Ireland

William Collins' dream of knowledge for all began with the publication of his first book in 1819.

A self-educated mill worker, he not only enriched millions of lives, but also founded a flourishing publishing house. Today, staying true to this spirit, Collins books are packed with inspiration, innovation and practical expertise. They place you at the centre of a world of possibility and give you exactly what you need to explore it.

© HarperCollins*Publishers* Limited 2020

10 9 8 7 6 5 4 3 2

ISBN 978-0-00-839761-6

Collins® and COBUILD® are registered trademarks of HarperCollins*Publishers* Limited

www.collins.co.uk/elt

British Library Cataloguing in Publication Data

A catalogue record for this publication is available from the British Library.

Author: Michaela Morgan
Illustrator: Laura Arias (Beehive)
Series editor: Rebecca Adlard
Commissioning editor: Zoë Clarke
Publishing manager: Lisa Todd
Product managers: Jennifer Hall and Caroline Green
In-house editor: Alma Puts Keren
Project manager: Emily Hooton
Editor: Barbara MacKay
Proofreaders: Natalie Murray and Michael Lamb
Cover designer: Kevin Robbins
Typesetter: 2Hoots Publishing Services Ltd
Audio produced by id audio, London
Reading guide author: Emma Wilkinson
Production controller: Rachel Weaver
Printed and bound by: GPS Group, Slovenia

MIX
Paper from
responsible sources

FSC
www.fsc.org

FSC™ C007454

This book is produced from independently certified FSC™ paper to ensure responsible forest management.

For more information visit: **www.harpercollins.co.uk/green**

Download the audio for this book and a reading guide for parents and teachers at www.collins.co.uk/839761